Clarion Books
a Houghton Mifflin Company imprint
215 Park Avenue South, New York, NY 10003
Text and illustrations copyright © 2005 by Clavis Uitgeverij Amsterdam-Hasselt.
Translation copyright © 2007 by Houghton Mifflin Company.

First published as *Benno buitengewoon* in Amsterdam-Hasselt in 2005
by Clavis Uitgeverij. First American edition, 2007.

The illustrations were executed in oils.
The text was set in 22-point LT Tapeside.

For information about permission to reproduce selections from this book, write to
Permissions, Houghton Mifflin Company, 215 Park Avenue South, New York, NY 10003.

www.clarionbooks.com

Printed in Italy.

Library of Congress Cataloging-in-Publication Data

Robberecht, Thierry.
[Benno buitengewoon. English]
Sam tells stories / by Thierry Robberecht ; illustrated by Philippe Goossens. — 1st American ed.
p. cm.
Summary: When Sam changes schools, he tells some pretty amazing stories about himself, but after a
few days, when he confesses that he is just boring, regular Sam, he finds that he still has friends—
and a talent that makes him more interesting.
ISBN-13: 978-0-618-73280-7
ISBN-10: 0-618-73280-2
[1. Honesty—Fiction. 2. Friendship—Fiction. 3. Storytelling—Fiction.] I. Goossens, Philippe, ill. II. Title.
PZ7.R53233Sam 2007
[E] —dc22
2006014382

12.00 7/07
Ingram 22952

10 9 8 7 6 5 4 3 2 1

Sam TELLS STORIES

by Thierry Robberecht

Illustrated by Philippe Goossens

Clarion Books

New York

I'm Sam.

I'm the most amazing kid in school.

The kids at my new school just don't

know it yet.

"My dad is an astronaut,"
I tell them on my first day.
"Is that true?" someone asks.
"Of course it's true. He flies to
the Moon and Mars and all over
the whole galaxy in his spaceship."

Everyone wants to be friends with me now.
They all wish they had an astronaut for a dad.

At home that night, my little brother
wants a bedtime story.
"Today a dragon visited our playground,"
I tell him. "It was a fire-breathing dragon!"

13

"Were you afraid?" he asks.

"No way. We chased him away with the garden hose," I say.

The next day at school,

everyone's talking about my dad.

A little too much, actually.

"Sam, has your dad flown to Mars lately?"

"Yes," I say. "He even met some aliens.

They came to our house for dinner!"

I'm starting to wish I hadn't told this story.

After school, I stay to play soccer
with my new friends.
By the time we're done, my clothes are a mess.
My mom is not happy.

19

"We had a fight with some of the big kids,"
I tell her. "They tried to take our lunchboxes!"
Mom is furious. But not at me.

Mom and Dad talk about the fight during dinner.
They're going to speak to my teacher!
"She should be taking better care of
the smaller children," Mom says.
I don't say anything.

That night, I can't sleep.

Everyone will know my stories aren't true.

My parents, my teacher, my friends.

"No more stories," I promise myself.

From now on, I'll just be Sam.

Boring, regular Sam.

At school the next day,
I tell my friends the truth.
They're not happy I lied to them.
"His dad isn't really an astronaut!"
"He made it all up!"
But after school, they still ask me
to play soccer.
I may not be the most amazing kid in school,
but I have amazing friends.

That night, my little brother wants to
hear about the dragon again.
"It was just a story," I tell him.
"It wasn't true."
"But you tell the *best* stories!" he says.
Maybe I'm not so boring after all.
I'm Sam, the most amazing storyteller ever.